Dream
Awake

Poetry & Prose

Sarah A. MacDonald

White Clover Publishing

Published by White Clover Publishing
Box 221, R.R.4
Echo Bay, Ontario
Canada P0S 1C0

ISBN-13: 978-0-986-66280-5
ISBN-10: 0-9866-6280-1

Library and Archives Canada Cataloguing in Publication

MacDonald, Sarah A., 1988-
Dream awake : poetry & prose / Sarah A. MacDonald.

ISBN 978-0-9866628-0-5

I. Title.

PS8625.D75285D73 2010 C811'.6 C2010-907252-9

Dream Awake

For my Father & Mother

Contents

Those who fear the imagination condemn it:
something childish, they say,
something monsterish, misbegotten.
Not all of us dream awake.
But those of us who do have no choice.

Patricia A. McKillip

Poetry

Dream Awake

When the living life has lost lustre
We have to dream awake

To make a place where
Words never spoken sound sweetest
And the words never written matter most
Where the memory of places you've never been
And people that never were start to become

Slowly, in all the things that aren't
You find reason

At times there's a calling, a warning for waking
That seeps like a throbbing into your land
But the yearning for forsaking triumphs
And each day that your minds takes to leaving
Brings you farther and further from Real

To continue dreaming sanity becomes an act
A well rehearsed shadow of a former self
And the more you turn reality into dream
The more you forget
Dreams that burn as bright as flame are consumed
By the fires blaze of light all the same

So you must ask
Are you willing to burn
For an empty brilliance?

Blue Angel King

Blending winter bird
Merging shadows
Melting snow
Flitting wing beats
Coarse call songs
I want for myself
The hidden angel king
Ruler of frosted forests

Sky and snow are blind
In seeing his gliding rush
And hover dances
So blind to him I set a trap
Strung on branch and body
A web of gilded metallic
Sparks off sunshine
And in cloud lies unseen

Blue jay now caught
In wire threads
Where he once flew
No longer sings
Royal purple seeps
Over blue feathers
Ripe berry red
Cancels downy white

The blue angel king
Now mine, is silent dead
Invisible no more
And though deposed
I have learned
His crown is one
That cannot be stolen
For this I despair

The Mailman

Someone killed the mailman.
They found him sprawled
On Mr. Moore's front lawn
After several calls about a vagabond passed out,
Made by Mrs. Andrews next door
Who enjoyed periodically peeking
Through lace curtains.

The sprinklers kept him moist,
Making tiny pink puddles
Everywhere that seeped
Into the sidewalk and settled.
They found his letters
Scattered across town,
Caught in trees and fences
They fluttered in the wind
With edges stained the brightest red.

Bumblebee glossed tape
Twisted in the breeze,
Coyly whispering "look here"
As the neighbour's Pomeranian
Scampered around the yard
With the dead man's black shoe.
Children laughed as he pranced
Around the crime scene,
Sticky red and puff white,
Like a dirty mall Santa.
I made note to myself
That black hides blood
So very well,
But white dogs do not.

The crowds gathered to glimpse
The man turned swiss cheese
And stained cherry bright,
While men in crisp uniform
Scurried from house to house,
Peering into windows,

Knocking on doors,
While hand lay butterfly
Over holstered metal.
Seems the man was shot several times,
His torso and head polkadot pierced
By drops of moulded mineral.

I told the officer that, perhaps,
It was a failed effort
To create a more aerodynamic mail carrier,
Or that dogs had finally escalated
In their acts of postman brutality,
Suggesting he look into the neighbour's dog,
Snowflake, who was currently savouring
His black leather trophy.
The officer's reply
Was the scuffle of footsteps
Gently attacking pavement.
Rise and fall, rise and fall,
The impatient foot betrays
The trained façade.

I ask him, "do you know the culprit?"
His face veiled
With mirror tinted glass
Hid the secret of his eyes
As he replied, "no suspects so far,"
While he turned to leave.

What of the mail?
He had gone before I could ask.
Left standing doorstep distraught
I worried for my missing mail,
For those envelopes that roamed splatter red,
And wondered if blood could be bleached
From bills and letters.

Cluttered street side
People hummed electric gossip,
As cars crawled
Baby slow in passing.

Betraying the pattern
A black sedan stopped,
Straddling sidewalk
Before the commotion.
A women burst out crying
While the car door swung teeter,
Squeaking and squealing -
As if mice hid in the hinges.

Rushing the scene
She tried to hopscotch
Over yellow tape,
And flutter past a battalion
Of grasping hands.
All this time the woman
Screaming, screeching,
"Mike! Mike!" Though "Mail! Mail!"
Was what I'd heard.

I found a comrade in the mourning
Of our misplaced mail,
Whose passion permeated
Through the people
Like emotional plague,
Wringing signs of pity,
Coaxing tears,
And squeezing sighs.

I would leave the task
Of the mail to her,
She, who made them understand
The importance of those errant
Letters that wandered stray.
They forget that mail trumps
A case of murder.
It's the mail first
They'll come to understand,
The mail before the mailman,
She'll make them understand.

Fire Fades

The flickered licks of soul's low fire fade
As heated tendrils wilt in waning light
A sigh for one more of the fallen prayed

Be silent breath of the now decayed
Another lost to hellish fire light
The flickered licks of soul's low fire fade

See bodies, each upon another laid
Their faces torn in shadows cry out plight
A sigh for one more of the fallen prayed

The virtuous few spared torment have strayed
For wicked darkness tempts this endless fight
The flickered licks of soul's low fire fade

A sea of bodies where the living wade
Its colour shaded in a black twilight
A sigh for one more of the fallen prayed

And we are left with no souls to bade
An empty breath of life, we fall to blight
The flickered licks of soul's low fire fade
A sigh for one more of the fallen prayed

Ancestral Hounds

Ancestral hounds bay
At a ripe moon and pregnant
Clouds that threaten rain

Crimson Clover

We found ourselves there as we slipped
Between the waking world and the dreaming
We forgot both and we remembered

Sitting in a field of crimson clovers
Plucking the fourth leaves
When found we devour them
Luck in the belly

Hands brush and caress, stirring red organic waves
A ginger, gentle touch, soon crudely interrupted
As hand hits hardness beneath the blushing clover
Clack, Clack - the tumble of dirty bones
Slumbering children fertilized, blood and flesh
"You are not here" their empty heads whisper
Again we hear, Clack, Clack
As their teeth chatter clumsy

We do not listen, shoving earth into our ears
And clover in our mouths
Gnaw and gnaw, bleeding warm
Sweetness seeping through tooth and tongue
We are frantic now
Find the fourths, look for luck

Crouching in our shadows panic prickles
Fear snarling in the hollows of our hearts
Sticky and heavy it slows the flutter of our time
Hurried hands gouge frantic fistfuls
Shovelling and stuffing them, quicker, into our mouths
Sweet red saliva drips down trembling chins
Torrents of clover fall from our stained lips
Earth falls from our ears
We fall from our straight standing

Clack, Clack - the bones are laughing as our bodies still
Clovers swish and sway from our plummet
We are left food for the fourths
We are not here

The Boy and The Birds

A small child shoots, "Bang, Bang!"
With a finger pistol
Aimed at the mother sparrow
Who wakes him every morning at six
With unwelcomed song

Her chicks chirp
And strain their necks
Bare of feathers
He turns and aims, "Bang, Bang!"
Making the baby birds fantasy dead

When his tabby, Mr. Whiskers
Brings the mother sparrow, dead
And her chirping chicks cry louder
The pistol is forgotten

The third morning after
Mother sparrow's death
He wakes at eight to silence
And fills the empty sound
With a sob-song all his own

The Circus

They took me to the circus
I found it very odd

The creature cries and
Bloodshot eyes hunted
Hungry after everyone

The crowds thunder-cheered
For the people clad in rhinestone dew
Topped with neon feathers
That flipped and tumbled in mid-air

I did not understand the fun
And couldn't help but point and say
That birds and angels had no cords
And animals were not born to be imprisoned

As my parents hushed and shushed,
The acrobat slipped, fell smack-crack
As his bone punctured suit and skin together

Then the crowds fell silent
And caged tigers began to riot
Fueled by blood and rage

Their cages, clasped, heaved open
And the big cats sprung into a frenzied run
As the spectators rushed to flee
Throwing cotton candy sweets
And other treats to perish
Under rows of trampling feet

And as my parents pulled and pushed me
Through the teaming-screaming crowd
I couldn't stop my childlike thought
The Circus was rather fun

Caged

Lyris was told she was a bird
She belonged in a cage
Locked

At first she did not believe
There could be a bird without
Wings and feathers
Beak and tail
Like she

But day and day
Night and night
She heard
"You are a bird"
She believed them

But birds are wild
Flighty free
When caged seek to soar
Lyris was a bird
Who yearned for flight
So when the cage was left askew
She darted out
Towards the window open wide

While she perched on the sill
Her caretakers cooed
"Here Dear, to the cage, to the cage"
But she was a bird
Who yearned for flight

She jumped high to fly
But instead tumbled and fell
With a sickly thud
Seven stories down

Because people are not birds
And lies are not truth
A once caged child dies

Hush Hush

Though you will lose
The silent struggle
You will have won

For all the raging
Of your life's light
That ebbs and fades
Into nothing
There is a mark
A remembrance
Of your burning
The ghost whisper
That remains though
You do not

So do not fret
And do not fear
I have been scorched
By your burning
With me you will live forever

Insane Love

Would you kill the ones you love to save them?
Would you kill someone you love because of love?
Ask for forgiveness?
Pray for forgiveness?
Long for a blessing when you're left alone?
Spiral faster, further, freer into depths of sin
Seek a damnation deserved in the darkness?

You realize have no choice
But to answer fading will
As your soul is torn to shreds
And your mind slips

To save the ones you love
You must destroy
All that harms and hurts
All that pains and suffers

You must destroy yourself to save them
Before you've lost
Control and sense
Before you've forgotten love
In the depth of a mind blasted hell

You decide you have to die
And you die alone
Because you've already taken love
And killed it

Resolve comes too late

Your loved ones already turned to demons
Souls high burning
Only set free with the slice of a blade
Held bloody and steel bright
The reflection shows
Your slowly turning devil too

You've lost
Turned to a blood sullied beast
That no longer knows
No longer cares
Forgotten human
In the swirl of confusion and madness
That chokes remnants of a soul
Left to dream of paper moons

There's nothing left to save

Goodbye Blue Sky

The sky in my mind is too perfect
The blue hue is too vibrant
And no wind whispers
And no bird song lingers
In the sky in my mind
That burns, burns, burns
Through what was once true

Wings of Children

Teeter tiptoe
Walk on high
Between
The perched and flighty bird
An imitation

Standing precariously on the tips of feet
Swaying unbalanced from side to side
Rising above slightly with each
Dainty
Step

Risking a falter and a fall
With every
Tender
Placed
Toe

Rising
Shifting
A bouncy walk that risks loss
The false flight of children
Before they forget innocence

As after imitated heights
They face the plummet
The
   Fated
      Fall

False

Nothing could change death's parade
People cried out for their salvation
They called me God and silently prayed

I sat upon a pretty throne displayed
While children cried alone, eyes swollen
Nothing could change deaths parade

The growing dead in alleyways decayed
While those still left spoke holy doctrine
They called me God and silently prayed

The fallen cities blazed demons jade
Thousands fell to frenzied famine
Nothing could change deaths parade

Anguished screams in night would fade
To those lingered, pressed with passion
They called me God and silently prayed

People fell, while the damned had stayed
Left to bathe in their festered sins ruin
Nothing could change deaths parade
They called me God and silently prayed

Azure Stars

Azure stars fall from heaven's heights
Plummeting intensity, mad rain
Perfect, misty blue hue
Illuminating brightly
Sputter-flicker in their fall

Translucent tails left in wake
Smudge the sky blue angel glow
Slow-quick fading into the night
Blending softly
We forget their splendour

These rain water stars
Seek to be remembered

Fall from high
Coming closer
Illuminate the Night
A beautiful blaze of ice-fire

They cannot remain
Burning brilliant

Darkness seeps into light
Flooding brightness with black
Every love-starved star dies

We are left an empty sky
Forgetting it was ever
Anything else

Savage Garden

There is a garden maintained unkempt
Sheltered by the gloating grey skies
That loom taunting rain
Smother sweet sunlight

There the vegetation is cannibalistic
Flowers feeding on grass
Weeds devouring flowers
Trees consuming weeds
Round and round the eating goes

But still they thrive through the fighting
Creeping through crevices
The wrought iron cage fails to contain
Seeds and saplings that yearn to escape and destroy

Every day the garden grows
As children crawl farther past their bounds
And grow, and grow, while they devastate
Those finely manicured lawns we keep tame

And the garden grows

Lilies Dance

Lilies dance on a
Misted pond and cool water
Reflects a ghost moon

Fallen

I'm not very white-light-bright anymore
My halo is floating farther away
These wings are torn to slight shreds
I can't save myself anymore
I think I've fallen

I'm dashed-out-dirty standing here
My prayers won't leave these lips
Trapped inside this tiny burnt out soul
Tears will not fall from my guilty eyes
I'll cry inside until I drown myself

Though these wings are broken
I want to flutter-fly again
I want to run higher to heaven
But this dropped down body won't move
So I'll say my silent lip locked prayers
To a heaven that hears, and has refused me

This soul is so strained and stained
That it doesn't shine or glitter glow
Still I'll keep praying, crying
No more flutter-flying
Till someone, someday, comes to save me

Greener Grass

While mowing my lawn
I hit a mole that rose from the earth
Inopportune timing for the
mini monster who ravaged
a would be manicured yard

The blades churned out
It's blended body
Covering the grass
In bloody-body bits

Within the next week
The grass grew greener
Neighbours marvelled at the
Lush and vibrant lawn

To keep the earthen tresses their finest
I searched for moles to turn to mulch
Keeping my ground well fed

Rapidly my mowers blades began to decay
Blood rusted and bones dulled
Once honed edges

As a rational creature I have decided
For the sake of my mower
To return to traditional fertilizer

Falter

There's an angel bound to a wooden chair
Someone I love, someone I've forgotten
Sitting skewed, sinister still, straight undone

This must just be another ephemeral dream
Where delicate late night lullabies of
Broken wings are whispered ever so small
Those precious darling songs sung in the waking

A name, a single word, has the power to rule
I want to call yours over and over
Sweetly and slowly until my mouth
Burns raw, but I can't remember it

There's a remedy, a sweet little pill
Called ignorance. Just another bit
Of downers logic - a fake magic spell

This must just be another cynical bad trip
Since we've got nowhere left to hide and the
People we had met and known are all just
Quietly chanting "ashes to ashes"
Like a prayer, such gentle praying words

As always God is watching us
Play our daily games, we say amen and then
It's time to say goodbye - leaving is what we do

Shooting Butterflies

The moon started dying, its life leaving, blood spilling. A thick silver mud smudged down the sky, trailing, trickling, and pooling at the bottoms of their feet - sticky and heavy, smelling of dirty lilies.

Throughout the night it bled metallic, like candle wax rippling and folding downwards. The moon was stuck still, pouring itself glossless grey, a matte mate of the darkening sky, the dead Goddess was lost, the despairing sun had followed within days.

A billion sputtered flames and it was tamed into a swiftly fading smear in the amber skies. Just a pale smudge of rouge, a reminder that heaven kissed the skies then left - ever the capricious lover.

The nights started bleeding over, as golden noons became burnt bloody skies, clotted blood growing darker, deeper red, hazy scarlet, stale maroon, and then daylight broke to black – the shatter of a sheltering sky.

The people were left with nothing above but the flicker of forsaking stars. A soundless protest as they chided their children for having loved these little sinners, guiltless gods of ruin that trounced on the husk of a dead child.

After the third day, without word or warning, the masses started peeling hunks of moist flesh from the surface, their agreement shown through filthy nails and the clang and bang of dirty shovels.

One by one, damp black gaping mouths opened, hours passing as the many graves were dug in fervour to the tune of symphonic screams.

Those who finished first laid themselves down to watch the remnants of a broken sky, muttering prayers, gently sobbing, then uttering only silence. Others fell in half-dug holes dead, twisted heaps at the bottom of a shallow grave, failures later favoured lucky, as those that lasted longest left behind less lovely corpses.

The survivors started tearing, digging, peeling at themselves until their fingers wore down to bone. Bloody pulped bodies sputtered laughter, shrill and mad, before joining the deceased.

Within hours millions had died, desperately gasping, hands dirt groping, flesh tearing - then, Silence. No clash of beating eyelids, tear and scrape of skin, or drone of wheezing breath. The absence became a lacking lullaby, a delicate song for the slumbering dead.

After mere minuets black brash butterflies crept from gaping mouths. Their flimsily powdered blades tearing at the air, wing pulses thrashing, a sweet powdered frenzy born from still warm corpses.

The silence broke with the thunder clash of battering wings, causing a torrent of tiny tremors that ruffled remnants of human hair and rippled pools of crimson mud.

Then the stopping started, a slowing of the flutter-beat, falling lower, soaring slower. Heartbeat skipped, then they dropped and dipped. A delicate crash and tumble of paper wings that turned to ash, settling soot for the open graves.

Ashes to ashes, dust to dust, and no one's left to pray.

All that remained was the darkly burning dawn and a quiet pockmarked surface. The lacking lullaby returned, and silence grew to embrace the end.

Prose

Nothing

She sat down on the worn, dirty carpet of her bedroom - the dust rising like falling streams around her tiny seven year old body. Pale gold hair framed her face in a loose tumble of waves, eyes a shining dull green were focused on her worn grey socks. With one already on her foot, she stretched out the second, poking her fingers through the little holes that littered the bottom. She didn't mind the holes as long as they were in places where no one could see. Pulling on the sock, she wiggled her toes, inspecting the growing hole from which her smallest toe was peeking. Then, tugging on her scuffed black shoes, she leapt to her feet, teetering for a moment before finding her balance and skipping into the tiny apartment's kitchen.

The fridge was broken again, other than her father's case of cheap beer, there was only a carton of expired milk. Thinking a bit of warm milk wouldn't be so bad, she swung the door open only to be assaulted with a sour whiff of stale air. She grabbed the carton with both hands and took a sip, only to spit it back out. It was chunky and the taste was nothing reminiscent of milk. Disappointed, she put it back in the fridge and closed the door. Then crawling headfirst into the mostly bare cupboard, she found a box of cereal which was nearly empty. Grabbing little fistfuls of stale flakes, she ate it from her hands, since all the bowls were sitting in the sink, dirty. Still hungry, she ran back to the cupboard to find a half-full jar of peanut butter. Scooping out a spoonful of the creamy brown feast she licked at it, much like a normal child would devour ice cream, or a popsicle.

Finished with her makeshift breakfast, she rushed to her mother's bedroom. Standing before the closed door she tapped gently. "Mama?" she called, then pushed the door open a crack. Peering into the shaded room she spotted her mother curled into a trembling ball, crumpled in the centre of a sagging, stained bed. Opening the door further she took a tentative step inside the dank room, whispering again, "Mama?" Her mother replied with a gentle, broken sob. "Mama, I'm going to school now... remember to eat, okay?" Her mother sobbed further, never looking up. Leaving the room and closing the door she murmured gently, "goodbye Mama" in a sombre tone.

*****

Walking home from school, she dodged the people who trod absentmindedly on the sidewalk. Battered briefcases and oversized purses roughly bumped her shoulders. Stopping in an empty alley she pulled out a little ornament from her pocket. It was a metallic golden flower, with tiny plastic bells, that fit in the palm of her hand. Her mother had thrown it at her some months before in a fit of sobbing hysteria, it only grazed her head, barely left a mark. She thought of it as a gift though, a good luck charm from her mother that she cherished. She rubbed the plastic petals against her cheek, the bells made a soft, dull clanking sound, the plastic leaves slightly scratched her skin. She shoved it into her pocket and ran back, onto the side walk, mingling with the crowd again. As she walked she kept her hand, hidden in her pocket, clasped tightly around her tiny treasure.

✱✱✱✱✱

"Mama, I'm home" she said through the empty sliver of open door. No reply. She closed the door quietly, a sad little smile played on her lips. She then walked towards the little living room and sat down in front of a fifteen-inch battered television set. Turning it on, the crackle of static burst through the silence. A fog of black and white illuminated the dimming room. Jumping to her feet she adjusted the bent bunny ears, the snow becoming fuzzy cartoon pictures. She spent the rest of the night perched in front of the screen, watched the colours, listened to the noise, enjoying the company of the artificial. When she had finally grown weary she made her way into her bedroom, her tiny feet dragging on the floor making a silent scratchy sound. She was too tired to say goodnight to her mother, neither did she want to wake her if she was sleeping. So she wandered into her bed, nesting in a lumpy limp pink comforter and rested her head on a bunched pillow.

✱✱✱✱✱

He came home after one a.m., kicked out of his favourite bar with nowhere else to go but home. He had run short on cash, adding to his never waning tab, again. He worked as a firefighter so he hadn't been home in weeks. He wasn't in any rush to return. His wife was shut up in their bedroom and the last time he left, she was screaming and crying. He didn't think his daughter was right either, she was the total opposite of her mother, but she wasn't right, mentally. She never cried or got angry - he didn't think that was proper. She never made any friends at school, hardly spoke to anyone, and always smiled – but never laughed. She was wrong, his whole family was.

✱✱✱✱✱

45

The lights filtered through her open door and rested on her once-slumbering face. Rubbing at her eyes she sat up in confusion. She had turned off the lights, and her mother hated anything bright. She climbed out of bed and peered past her door. She heard the hum and buzz of the television, then saw her father's head above the sofa. She burst from her room and smiled as she ran towards her father.

"Daddy! I knew you'd come today" She smiled more, but he only glanced without comment.

"Daddy, I'm so happy you remembered, really happy!" she said still smiling.

"Remembered what?"

"My birthday, that's why you came home, right? It was sooo late!! But you surprised me, I'm so happy." Her smile grew wider.

"Huh? Oh, right, sure. How old are you this time?" He asked, slightly surprised.

"I'm seven now!" she said holding up seven fingers so he could see.

"Oh, that's great, you're getting old." He walked to the fridge and opened it. "God! What's with that smell?! The beer's not even cold." He grabbed the clinking case and walked back to the living room.

"It's broken, it stopped working last week, you shouldn't drink that – it might be chunky too." She pointed to the open bottle of beer in his hand.

"It's fine, just warm. Go to bed."

She stood staring at him, still smiling. "But Daddy, you're my present! I don't want to go to bed. If I do you'll disappear..."

Her smile faded.

He was glad she had stopped smiling; relieved he pulled out a handful of caramel candies from his pocket, "here, these can be your present, go to bed now."

Snatching them from his hands she ran back into her room, placing them beside her pillow so she could watch them while she slept.

✳✳✳✳✳

She stood in front of the couch, her father passed out, beer bottles scattered around him.

"I'm going to school now, Daddy. I'm glad you stayed for me! I bet your tired from my birthday surprise, I really liked it. Bye Daddy, I love you."

She kissed his forehead then ran out the door. The streets were busy, people crowded the sidewalks and the blare of car horns drowned other sounds. She pulled out one of the candies her father had given her. She held it in the centre of her hand as she walked, her gaze fixated on the little brown cube. She smiled warmly and whispered "Daddy's gift" to herself. She walked slowly through the crowd, holding the candy close to her body. Walking through a dirty crosswalk she was bumped by someone rushing past her, her candy tumbled from her grip and onto the pavement below. Rushing towards it, she crouched down and picked it up gingerly, then hugged it in her hands. No one was walking anymore; she wondered where all the people went as she rose from the ground, her candy clutched in her hand. Then suddenly, there was nothing.

✳✳✳✳✳

Tiny drops fell onto the pavement beside her face.

"Oh, it's raining," she whispered to herself. She wondered why the rain only fell near her face and nowhere else. Then, she realized it was coming from her eyes. She brought a trembling hand to her face, feeling the tiny river that crept down her cheek. "Mama, me too, I think I'm sick too – look, my eyes are raining." Her hand fell gently to the ground, "I'm cold, I'm tired. Mama – when's the rain going to end?" She fell unconscious, tears still seeping from her closed eyes.

✳✳✳✳✳

47

The two men sat across from each other, not knowing what to say. One an elderly man, haggard from age and slouched in his chair, the other with bloodshot eyes and the scent of rancid beer on his breath. They both sat in a dull white room, reeking of antiseptic, waiting to hear what the status of the little girl was, if she was going to even live.

Suddenly the old man barked, "What the hell is wrong with you! She's your daughter, for God sakes! You sure as hell ain't no son of mine."

The old man stared at him, seething. "What do you have to say for yourself? She's dying dammit and you're still drunk off your ass! She'd be fine if you weren't such a failure."

Her father lifted his head and looked at the old man, his eyes red and glossed from a hangover. Yelling, his father screamed, "What do you have to say?! Say something dammit, what do you have to say!?!" Her father looked up and spoke in a dry voice, "What can I say? There's nothing." and hung his head again.

*****

Beep, beep, a man stained ripe cherry red stood before him, "Sir, your daughter is... there's nothing we can do for her. I'm sorry."

Then the slowing of the heart monitor's beep, again the blood stained man, "Sir..? Is there anything I can do for you?" followed by a harsh mechanical hiss.

"Uh, the mother, her mother."

"Pardon?" The red man asked confused.

"Tell her, shouldn't you? I can't, just can't."

"Yes, of course, I'll contact her for you."

The hiss stopped and the red man went back behind the swinging doors, voices slipping through with the swoosh as they flapped back and forth, "Abigail Brenton, time of death..." and the door closed.

Hide and Seek

The small boy tugged on the frayed edges of his
mother's skirt, whining, "Mommy, I'm hungry... Mommy!"
"Hush, be quiet. I'm making something right now.
Why don't you go play?" He lifted his head towards his
mother, his face delicate and feminine, his curly hair shaded
dirty sunshine.
"But I want to wait with Mommy!" His wide glassy
green eyes pleaded, his hands were wound in his mother's
skirt, kneading and pawing at the fabric flowers.
"No, I'm busy. Get out!" She shoved the little boy
away.
"Mommy?"
"Just go, please, Mommy is very busy" Her eyes
became wet and pink with her words. "Please? Just go."
"Okay, I'll play outside."

As his mother turned, he ran through the house,
bursting onto the deck made of wood, rough and rotting,
careful with his steps. Tight tremors in his chest made him
stop, coughing violently his ashen face turned bright pink. A
small girl sitting on the edge of the porch turned towards

him, "Mom told you not to run! Geez your soo dumb! You know you're not supposed to, you're always sick, sick, sick..." She dangled her legs over the edge, her face turned towards her flicking feet.

"I know! Don't tell Mommy! Please, I don't want her to get more mad at me!" He yelled quietly, trying to catch his breath.

The blond girl waved her hand at him, still looking at her feet. Satisfied, he wandered towards the opposite side, slowly sitting on the dirty wood. He pulled a tiny, ragged olive-green book from his pocket and perched it in his lap. Sounding out letters and whispering random words he read from the water stained pages. An older version of the little boy walked up the steps and paused in the doorway, stepping backward, looking at the cross-legged child.

"Shesh, you can't even read, give it up – your pathetic." After a lingered look he disappeared into the cabin. Pouting, the younger boy whispered a story to himself, his eyes skimming over the faded text, his fingers gently gripping the worn cover.

"You can eat now!" His mother shouted from within.

Jumping to his feet he shoved his book back into his pocket. Walking quickly he burst into the room, his face scrunching in response to the smell of supposed supper.

"Yuck! I don't want to eat that!" he shouted.

"You have to eat, it's very important," his mother muttered.

"But Mommy, it's icky!"

"Just eat it, please, just for tonight... eat it for Mommy, okay?" Her voice quivering.

"Alright, just for today! I'll eat for Mommy. You'll be happy right?"

"Yes, right, I'm happy." She whispered without looking at him.

Climbing onto the stool he sat before the sparsely laid table. His sisters across, his brothers on either side, and his mother, at the head, sat silently before an empty plate while the children ate. The bowl was filled with murky brown water and various lumps of leftovers. He plunged his spoon into the bowl, hungry, and ate.

 ✶✶✶✶✶

Gently shaking his body, his mother cooed, "Caleb, Caleb, wake up."

"Mommy?" He rubbed his eyes.

"Get up honey, we're going for a walk in the woods."

"Huh? But it's still dark! Is everyone coming?"

"No, it's just going to be me and you, a special walk." She grabbed his hand gently, leading him outside.

"Just me and Mommy? Really?" His eyes glistened.

Her vision fixed on the path before them. "Yes, just you and me..."

✶✶✶✶✶

Standing on a patch of brown and moss speckled grass he wiggled his toes, grasping for the green peeking from beneath. His mother kneeled feet away from him in a dry-dirt space. She pressed a broken twig into the ground, moving it in a circle around her body, stepping out of the ring she waved for her son to come. He ran smiling towards his mother, his hand aiming for hers was left lonely as she lifted it away. He let his hand hover where his mother's once was, grasping the air weakly.

"Mommy?"

"Here, stand in the circle I made, here in the middle." She shoved him into the dirt drawn ring, and then stepped backwards.

"Were going to play a game. It's called hide and seek. You stay here in the circle and wait for me to come find you. Whatever you do, don't leave the circle, ok?" Her eyes were drawn to her feet.

"So I just stand here and don't leave? Then Mommy will come find me?"

"Right, yes, don't leave the circle." She turned and stood still for a moment, almost looking back, then ran into the darkness, beyond his sight. Sitting in the dirt he took out

53

his ragged book, whispering a story into the night, but the dark, dense forest ate his words, so that no one could hear the boy who waited.

Waiting

Elie will be here soon. I'm sure of it. Until then, I look outside at the world... and wait. Admittedly, the view is boring and dull, but I'm hopeful that something of interest will eventually happen, that she will come. You will get the idea of what kind of place this is when I tell you that they call my residence Drawlson Homes, the name itself is lazy and dull, the home itself is a magnification of that, let me elaborate.

It's a plain one-story building, situated as far from civilization as possible. The exterior is a faded honey yellow colour, slathered over burnt bricks. The blistered paint is chipped and peeling in too many places. The building is shaped like a crudely drawn U, each room has a single small square window - grimy with filth. Its wooden frame is covered sloppily in flaking once white paint. When the wind blows, it seeps through the cracks like a cruel, chilling poison that sinks into the bones and settles painfully. The windows are a joke, since they don't even open, having been painted shut, surely in an effort to save time and money.

There is sparse landscaping outside - no trees or flowers, just brown patches of malnourished grass and the occasional dot of dry green. Weeds of every variety poke through the chipped cement walkway, becoming the most interesting part of the barren scenery. In the distance, the outline of the city belches smoggy clouds from its factories, and a blaze of light on the horizon refuses to surrender to the inky night.

The interior of the home is just as desolate. The lobby doubles as a sitting room, with only a large counter-like desk for the receptionist and a small, mint green sofa. There is a large window alongside the double doors, where people like to sit and watch for coming family members - it's also the cleanest window in the whole building. The view outside is still bleak, especially if you have no visitors.

The individual rooms of Drawlson aren't much better, every tiny cell-like room is the same. The cheap doors squeal with a harsh wail that makes the ear wince. A worn, filthy beige carpet is strewn childishly across the floor, bunched in some places, worn in others. The pea green wallpaper is frayed at the edges and torn bare in some.

Every room basically has the same sad contents, the sagging bed that squeaks in protest with every movement, the tacky metal arc of its headboard reminiscent of a jail cell. The mattress is thin and stained, the sheets were white, but are now cream coloured. Mine, though, are a faded mustard yellow. The pillows are limp and lumpy from overuse, and some have stains and spots of an unknown sort. As well every room has a small stout dresser of bare wood, with drawers that are impossible to open or shut, which one might have to pry open manually despite the crippled state of their hands.

Every room has a small khaki-coloured toilet, a chipped sink and tub. Some rooms have a small cracked mirror caked with years of stain, some don't. There's a nightstand of simple construction, basically just four pieces of wood glued together, and a plain white lamp on top. The light bulbs sputter and flicker, miming us, or so it seems with passing time.

So much for my accommodations!

I've been here for about a month but I don't plan on staying for very long. My daughter dropped me off in October. Now, it's mid November. I expect this arrangement is only temporary, I may be an old man, but I'm still capable of taking care of myself. The only reason I'm here is because my daughter had to sell my house and didn't have room for me. She said I had no use for it ever since my wife Lily died - too much space for one old man she told me, which makes sense (sort of). When I get out, I plan on finding something smaller, maybe a quaint little suburban house with lots of yard, nothing too fancy. I'd have it painted white, even if it already is. Lily always liked a freshly painted house. I doubt I'd go so far as to put up a white picket fence though. Hell, I might even get myself a dog. Ever since Lily went last year, I've felt incredibly lonely. Without her, everything seems too silent, the shadows too dark, the air bitter and stale. I suppose that's just me missing her.

Soon my Elie, my only child, will come and get me out of this place. I know she doesn't have the money to put me in one of those nicer homes, but I'm certain she could afford a place better than this. She has a family to raise, little Beth should be turning five in January - or was it seven? I'm not very fond of her husband; I'd rather not think about him. I wouldn't mind just her and Beth coming today. I miss having someone to talk with. I really don't like this place at all. It has a dead and empty feeling. I haven't bothered to make any friends yet, nor will I, since I'm bound to be leaving soon. Besides at my age there's no point in making friends – they'll just die like Lily.

I've been through many things in my long life. I've endured many hellish hardships - but right now, I can't imagine a worse place. It's draining, slow, and painful. I have a hard time remembering my past now. My memory seems more vacant than it once was. I guess that's bound to happen to anyone once they get a little older. Being in this place doesn't help my mind much, though Elie should be here to rescue me soon.

*****

Another month has passed, more life lost, time forgotten. The temperature is much colder—inside and out. A thin layer of snow covers the ground. The edges of the windows are tinted with frost. I still haven't heard from Elie. I'm starting to think I never will. I sit here, like I have for the past three weeks, in a hard wooden chair beside the window in my room, staring aimlessly through the filth of the pane... waiting.

My shrivelled hands are clasped tight in one another, and my head is cocked to one side. Today I can see my reflection, an old man with vivid white hair, no longer as thick as it was a few months ago. I'm not balding yet, my hair is just sparse in some parts. My face is more wrinkled, seeming to sag lower while the folds of limp skin have increased. My once twinkling blue eyes have turned flat and listless, my mouth drooping at the corners, my eyelids lower. I look as if I've aged ten years being here. My soul feels even older. I take my meals in my room now; I just don't feel like leaving the meagre comfort of my familiar setting. I mostly pick at the unpleasant meals, only taking a few bites. I've lost fifteen pounds. The nurse tells me that's bad, but I can't help it - I just don't feel like eating. But they really don't care about my health. They just want money, and as long as I'm alive, no matter how pitifully, they'll be happy.

I had never noticed the details of the window as

60

much as I do now, every green-brown stain that rims the edges, all the little cracks and scratches, even the flecks of paint flaking away, every one of the imperfections. Sometimes I peel away the layers of dirty white paint to pass time, scratching until the bare wood begins to splinter and peel back, but mostly I sit gazing out the window, searching for something... waiting. I spend almost every waking moment sitting at the window, looking for that unknown thing that I have so much faith in, so much hope for. I look, perhaps, because I have nothing to do but look, or maybe I look for something non-existent to give me hope. There's nothing else to do, I don't want to play chess with some other withered being who can't even remember how to move the knight, or listen to the stories of a hopeless woman about the "good old days." I'm already depressed as it is, and don't need to have the weight of others to bare.

*****

Finally! Yesterday Elie called me. She said she would come for a visit soon. Everything seems to have changed since she called. It's been better, brighter. The snow has thawed and the sun has been appearing more often, it's simply wonderful. I feel different now, happy I suppose, since I have something to look forward to. What matters is that she's finally coming, she's coming. I've been eating more now, but still in my room. If I ate anywhere else I'd feel a little lost. The food is still bland and tasteless, but it has a familiar, comforting embrace. I've started reading the paper again as well, looking at the real-estate section mostly. I even found a modest home for forty thousand. It's a one level plain thing with two bedrooms, the second room, of course, would be for Elie and Beth. It's small and cheap, but it's enough to satisfy my simple needs.

Staring out the window this morning, I noticed a

small white flower blooming near my window, possibly the first flower to bloom here. Each petal looks silky and smooth, unravaged by time and elements, a new white, unlike the dull and worn shades found elsewhere. I sit like I used to beside my window, but now I like to watch the small flower through the day, seeing the petals open in the morning and close in the evenings, just to simply watch the tiny changes. It's so elegant in its solitary manner, sitting alone in a patch of barren soil - the most beautiful of its type, and the only.

*****

Today I left my room for the first time because Elie is coming, I'm sure of it. I had a nurse wheel me to the large window at the entrance of the home so I could see when she came. I must admit I've been anxious, unsure of what my daughter's visit would bring today. She never told me what time she would be coming, so I went to the window around seven. I was the only one sitting there through the day, which suited my mood best, I was too excited to deal with the ramblings of some incompetent, withered person. I sat looking ruefully, lusting for someone to talk too, just to see them, just to be near them - someone that I know, that I love. If only to hear them breathe and share that same breath – I would be content.

So I sat there watching the road in the distance, squinting so I could almost clearly see. At first nothing passed the home, or even ventured close. After a few hours, I was getting slightly restless, my impatience growing, until an older red car came into view. Slowing, it turned into the parking lot and someone stepped out, at first I was unable to see who it was, but in my heart I knew that it was her, my Elie. I sat straight in my ridged chair, fixing the worn blue blanket on my legs. As I peered with excitement at the coming figure, I felt slightly disappointed that she never brought Beth with her, but I'm so desperate now for anyone familiar, I suppose it doesn't matter. The faceless figure suddenly came into view dashing my heightened hopes. It was only one of the nurses coming to work, not Elie. But in that same instant hope came rushing back into my mind, drowning the heavy disappointment. It was only noon. She had enough time left to come, even if it was only for a little bit, even if she wasn't going to bring me home. So I sat and waited patiently, staying beside the window until eight at night. A nurse wheeled me back to my room to sleep. I protested, attempting to explain to her that my daughter would be coming soon, but she said nothing - I feared her silence. I went to bed that night imagining the endless tragedies my daughter may have faced, praying she was safe and well.

*****

I knew that she would come for me soon, she never called to say anything about her delay, but I knew she would come, I knew. So I went every day to the window waiting for her. Every car that passed made my heart flutter in intense hope, only to be crushed by it speeding past, or being everyone, except Elie.

I would imagine the things we would talk about, how she would look, everything about that meeting. I sat for days at the window listless, I would spend almost my entire waking hours looking out past the glass... waiting. Those few days changed to a few weeks, and I began to worry about her, wondering why she wasn't here. Eventually, a nurse came to me on the seventeenth day, telling me that I should stop sitting there, that my daughter wouldn't come for me, that I should just stop. I told her to wait though, that Elie would

63

come today, this day, I told her to wait and see - Elie would come. But she never came. The nurse was right. The next day I stayed in my room.

Maybe she thinks I am dead, or maybe I'm just not worth her trouble. That day caused me the most pain I've ever felt. Am I unworthy of her time, was I going to spend the rest of my life here? Would I die alone in a place so foreign to me, where I knew no one and no one cared if I died? I felt numb. That is the day I died. There was nothing left, nothing. I was forgotten.

*****

I had a dream a few nights later, both splendid and startling. I was young again, in my twenties, standing in some solitary place alone. It was night, the moon was hovering in the inky sky, almost close enough to touch. I could see every small pit and crater, every speck of dust settled on its surface. The light was pouring off in slight wisps with a silver hue, soaking every surface in a clean light. A damp fog clung to the earth with desperation, thin and frail, with a faint transparency that let the earth peek through. Fresh blades of emerald grass tickled the subtle mist, tips drenched in a sweet smelling liquid.

I was standing in a clearing surrounded by lofty trees, simply lost in the wonder of the plain beauty resonating from this unknown place. Then the fog cleared further until nothing was left of it, and suddenly a small lake appeared in the distance. The water was smooth and black, I walked towards it with growing curiosity and peered into its depths, wondering what could possibly lurk below.

I leaned forward to touch the queer water, it was thick and heavy, slowly falling from my fingers and dripping into the lake below, never making a sound or ripple, the

64

smoothness of the water staying. Then suddenly I was in the lake, drowning, falling away from the surface. I sunk slowly through the folds of velvet water, gazing through the layers and resting my vision on the radiant moon above. As I sunk lower the light began to fade until I was bathed in the blackness completely.

I've been thinking about it for some time now since I've little left to occupy my thoughts with. I'm not sure what it meant, if it meant anything, but it left me ecstatic and desolate. The beauty of the scene was refreshing, and the lake a comfort as I fell farther into its depths. But it was only a dream, a reminder of a freedom I no longer I have, a life I no longer possess. I have nothing to look forward to, nothing left to hope for that won't be shattered.

So I'm left sitting at my window once more, starring out into the unseen. Even my flower, that which I cherished so much in these past mournful days, is beginning to wither. Every petal is now singed a sickly yellow around the edges and curled back in a cruel snarl. Many of petals have already fallen to the dusty earth, scattered now by a ruthless wind. I don't have anything left in this world anymore, nothing at all. I am utterly alone.

It's been a month since I last left my room to wait for Elie, a month since I realized the truth. Now I know that I'm truly alone in this filth ridden home with no escape, no hope. No one is coming for me - I'm going to die here.

When the nurse brings my food I prod the potatoes, moving them from side to side. Once I'm sure she's left I pick the cold metallic tray up and slowly make my way to the bathroom, gingerly sliding the food into the toilet with a tarnished fork, flushing the mess. When she comes back to retrieve the tray, she knows I've been a good boy. I do the same with my meds. I've decided there is no point in taking something that will prolong my suffering.

*****

It's been months since I've stopped eating, or at least that's how it feels. It's only been a few days, a week at most, since then, but it all seems slow, dimmer, time now is still and eerie, calm and mocking. The air now is overwhelming and thick, I'm gasping for it, but there is less every time. My heart is fluttering, beating forcefully within my chest - still all is slower, almost stopped completely. Stopped? That was it, I had slowed, now I've stopped. This was it, my release, my final resting and as I close my eyes, I know that Elie has come, and I no longer need... to wait.

About the Author

Sarah A. MacDonald holds a Bachelor of Arts (Honours) from Laurentian University in English and a Bachelor of Education from Nipissing University. *Dream Awake* is her debut work. She currently lives outside of Sault Ste. Marie.